A Huntsman Spider In My House...

Michelle K Ray

Illustrated by Sylvie Ashford

Morgan James
The Entrepreneurial Publisher™

Kids

NEW YORK

A Huntsman Spider In My House

Published in New York, New York, by Morgan James Publishing. Morgan James and The Entrepreneurial Publisher are trademarks of Morgan James, LLC. www.MorganJamesPublishing.com

The Morgan James Speakers Group can bring authors to your live event. For more information or to book an event visit The Morgan James Speakers Group at www.TheMorganJamesSpeakersGroup.com.

BitLit
FOR ALL THE BOOKS YOU OWN

FREE eBook edition for your
existing eReader with purchase

_____

PRINT NAME ABOVE

For more information,
instructions, restrictions, and
to register your copy, go to
www.bitlit.ca/readers/register
or use your QR Reader to scan
the barcode:

ISBN 978-1-61448-842-2 paperback
ISBN 978-1-61448-843-9 eBook
ISBN 978-1-61448-844-6 audio
Library of Congress Control Number:
2013952207

Cover Design by:
Bernadette
bskok@ptd.net

Interior Design by:
Bonnie Bushman
bonnie@caboodlegraphics.com

In an effort to support local communities, raise awareness and funds, Morgan James Publishing donates a percentage of all book sales for the life of each book to Habitat for Humanity Peninsula and Greater Williamsburg.

Get involved today, visit
www.MorganJamesBuilds.com.

Habitat
for Humanity®
Peninsula and
Greater Williamsburg
Building Partner

For children and
critters alike.

Acknowledgement

From Michelle

'With many thanks to my gorgeous and talented illustrator Sylvie; Angella and Bob for their ongoing faith and support; my family, Mum, Dad, Nat, Tone, Luke, Tara, Kerrie and Jacq for always being there; my girlfriends, Viv, EK & Kris for real life inspiration; Virginia for your quirky cool and Jeremy for your strength and commitment to action. Finally to Scott Frishman and all the family at Morgan James Publishing – I love you guys!'

From Sylvie

'Thank you to Pamela and John for always believing in me. Thanks to Johnnie and Ash for fuelling my imagination and thanks to Rosie for being my art buddy for so many years. Last but not least, thank you to Jeremy for being my constant encouragement.'

This Book Belongs To

....

There is a Huntsman spider in my house.

He is big and brown and hairy.

He is sitting high up on my bedroom wall looking very scary.

I am too afraid to go to sleep while he creeps around.

Oh my goodness he's crawled from the wall, right onto the ground.

I wish his hairy legs would walk him right out my front door.

Then I won't have to look at him, no not anymore.

I could squash him with my shoe, but he's not hurting me.

He's simply hunting insects, looking happy to be free.

What if I catch him carefully and release him out the door.

The Huntsman spider in my house wouldn't bother me no more.

He could live to see another day as Mother Nature intends.

Maybe some day the Huntsman Spider will become my friend.

Huntsman Spider Facts

Spiders are the most widely distributed venomous creatures in Australia, with an estimated 10,000 species inhabiting a variety of ecosystems, from our cities to the bush.

Spiders tend to incite more fear than favour, provoking phobias for some. Many visitors to our Aussie shores are more than a little worried about our venomous eight-legged friends.

While it is true we have some of the most venomous spiders in the world, Australia's spider reputation is bigger than its bite: records show no deaths from spider bites since 1981.

Huntsman Spiders belong to the Family Sparassidae and are widespread in Australia. They are famous for being scary, hairy, black/brown spiders with a leg span of up to 15cm.

In reality, they are reluctant to bite. A Huntsman Spider is more likely to run away when approached and their venom isn't considered dangerous for humans.

They are often discovered in cars, terrifying drivers by jumping out from their hiding space, whilst driving.

Despite their large size and speed, Huntsman Spiders are allies in the house as they help with pest-control by eating smaller insects. Importantly they are far less life-threatening than snakes or sharks, or even bees.

For more information on Huntsman Spiders go to;

http://australianmuseum.net.au/Huntsman-Spiders

http://www.australasian-arachnology.org/

Colour In

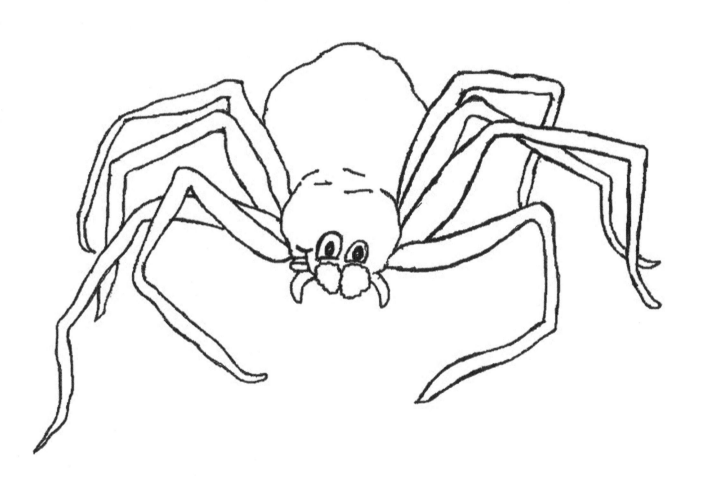

CPSIA information can be obtained at www.ICGtesting.com
Printed in the USA
BVOW10s1549160714

359386BV00005B/9/P

9 781614 488422